Published and distributed by

 ISLAND HERITAGE
P U B L I S H I N G
99-880 IWAENA STREET, AIEA, HAWAII 96701-3202
PHONE: (808) 487-7299 • FAX (808) 488-2279
EMAIL: hawaii4u@pixi.com

ISBN# : 0-89610-353-6

First Edition, Third Printing - 2000

THE LITTLE
HAWAIIAN RAINBOW

By Stacey Daum
Illustrated by Yuko Green

Dedication

For the little rainbow in my life, Shantessa

Long, long ago on the islands of Hawaii, way before people lived there, the land was dull. Everything on the islands was gray — the flowers, ocean, even the animals.

One day dark clouds covered all the islands and it started to rain. Not just any rain ... this was a special rain, a magical rain.

It rained for many days, until all of a sudden it just stopped.

The sun came out and shone over the islands, and when it did . . .

. . . the most wonderful
thing happened.

3

A beautiful rainbow appeared!

All of the animals and plants were amazed. They couldn't believe their eyes. They had never seen a rainbow before. They had never even seen colors before.

The Little Rainbow was very proud of himself. He wanted to show off all of his beautiful colors.

He set out to make some friends.

4

"Hello, Mr. Sun! How are you today?" asked The Little Rainbow.

"I am okay, I guess, but I would be much better if I had beautiful colors like you to brighten my day," said the gray, gray sun.

The Little Rainbow thought about it and decided to give the sun his yellow. The sun was so happy and proud he shone brighter than ever.

This made The Little Rainbow feel very good inside. He wanted to make more friends.

He saw a palm tree.

"Hello, tree! How are you today?" he asked.

"Oh, I'm afraid I haven't been feeling well lately. I'm getting old and my branches aren't what they used to be," said the gray, gray tree.

The Little Rainbow wanted to help. He remembered how he cheered up the sun when he gave him a color from his rainbow, so he decided to give the tree a color, too.

The tree felt so good in his new green color, he straightened up his trunk and stretched out his branches.

"I feel like a brand new tree! Thank you, Little Rainbow!" he said.

7

The Little Rainbow smiled and went to look for more friends. This time he came across an unusual looking flower called a bird of paradise.

"Hello, flower! Why do you look so sad?" he asked.

"None of the other flowers want to play with me because they think I look scary," said the gray, gray flower.

"I bet if I gave you a color you would look beautiful," said The Little Rainbow. "How about orange?"

The bird of paradise suddenly became radiant with its bright orange crown.

When the other flowers saw how beautiful she was, they all wanted color too. The Little Rainbow thought that was a great idea . . .

So he gave the gray, gray orchids **purple**, and he gave the gray, gray roses pink.

9

Smiling and gliding along, The Little Rainbow saw a gray, gray crab on the sea shore. Just as The Little Rainbow was about to say *HI*, a bird who wasn't watching where he was going almost stepped on the crab.

"That was close! Are you okay?" asked The Little Rainbow.

"I'm used to it," said the crab, "It happens all the time."

The Little Rainbow decided to give the crab his bright red color so that the crab could be easily seen. Then no one would step on him any more.

The crab was so grateful that he ran up and down the beach showing everyone his new color.

The Little Rainbow was having such a good time sharing all of his beautiful colors that he didn't notice he only had one color left.

As he floated over the ocean, he gave it a kiss of **blue**, and then disappeared into the sky.

The plants and animals saw he was gone and became very sad.

"Now we will never see our Little Rainbow or his beautiful colors again," they said.

The sun just smiled and told them to look around.

"The Little Rainbow may have gone away for now . . .

but
he left his beautiful colors in all of us."

"Hawaii is a rainbow!"

To this day only a few people know how Hawaii got all its beautiful colors.

And now you know too.

PAU!